If Raleigh Could Talk..... about Spring

Lindy Deusner

If Raleigh Could Talk..... about Spring

iUniverse books may be ordered through booksellers or by contacting:

iUniverse
1663 Liberty Drive
Bloomington, IN 47403
www.iuniverse.com
844-349-9409

ISBN: 978-1-6632-2940-3 (sc)
978-1-6632-2941-0 (e)

Library of Congress Control Number: 2021922954

Print information available on the last page.

iUniverse rev. date: 10/27/2021

To: Emma, Logan, and Luka

and their parents.

Jennifer, Beau, Elissa and Michelle

– and for all the dogs we have loved.

A Preschool Story Book

If Raleigh Could Talk...About Spring

Verse by Lindy Deusner – Drawings by Dennis Deusner

Copyright 2021

If Raleigh could talk,

he'd certainly say,

it's an awesome blue sky

and sunshine today.

If Raleigh could talk,

he'd want you to see,

the colorful blooms on

flowers and trees.

If Raleigh could talk

he'd want to share,

the grass is so green,

you won't have a care.

If Raleigh Could talk

he'd tell you some more,

about a new cardinal family

outside his door.

If Raleigh could talk
he'd tell you it's fun,
to sit on the deck and
soak up in the sun!

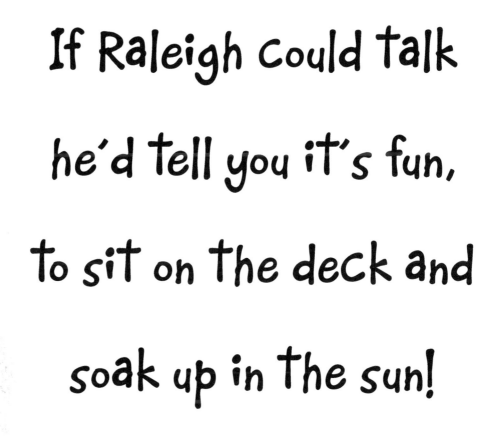

If Raleigh could talk

he'd say water is cool,

and whenever you like,

he'll jump in your pool!

If Raleigh could talk
he'd want you to know,
that ball sitting there,
he'd want you to throw.

If Raleigh could

talk he'd say

head down the street,

there's lots to explore,

dogs and people to meet.

If Raleigh could talk

he'd share this with you,

that the people inside,

he cares about too.

If Raleigh could talk,

I know he would say,

Get up! Go outside!

Have a Wonderful day!!

CPSIA information can be obtained
at www.ICGtesting.com
Printed in the USA
BVHW062259081221
623532BV00003B/21